BABY
CARROTS

BABY CARROTS

Carrots of Wisdom for Little Ones

Ten short tales from Henry the Great Blue Heron,
told in the garden, where his critter friends play, laugh,
and learn life's lessons along the way.

Written by SONDRA PERRY

Illustrated by Janice Byer

Edited by Jennifer Redovian

TWO HARBORS PRESS

minneapolis, mn

Two Harbors Press
322 First Avenue N, 5th floor
Minneapolis, MN 55401
612455.2293
www.TwoHarborsPress.com

Illustrated by Janice Byer
Edited by Jennifer Redovian
Cover Design by Mary Ross
Typeset by Kristeen Ott
Photo of Henry the heron on the last page taken by Sondra Perry

A portion of every book sold will go to the
Shepherd's Gate Shelter for Women and Children in Livermore, California.

www.KidsCarrotsBookSeries.com

ISBN-13: 978-1-62652-608-2
LCCN: 2014905512

Distributed by Itasca Books

Printed in the United States of America

To Samantha, my muse.

Contents

Introduction

I am Henry the Great Blue Heron, here in the Perry family's backyard. I am a bird. A very big bird. I am bigger than any hawk or eagle, but not as big as a dinosaur. I am four feet tall, and when I fly, my wings stretch six feet wide. It's true. Really!

My eyes are yellow. I have a white cap of fur on my head that sometimes sticks straight up. My feathers are mostly blue and gray. Some are brown and white. My beak is like a long, sharp spear, which is great for fishing. I also eat snails and gophers.

I live nearby, but most of the time you can find me in the Perry's backyard. I have been coming here almost every day for over ten years now. You see, this is a really special backyard! I love to hang out in the garden. The sun seems to always shine, and the flowers are always in bloom. It is a happy place. There is plenty of food and water, and I feel very safe. Birds and critters from the neighborhood are always flying or crawling into the Perry's yard. The Perry family takes good care of us all.

My friends are here too! There is the frog family, the lizard family, turtles, red robins, worms, turkeys, Mr. Duck, Baby Squirrel, blue jays, quails, and doves. Many little songbirds, and the three hens, Mother, Raven and Braveheart, live here too.

Whether they are eating, laughing, playing, or sometimes fighting, the critters are learning about themselves, those around them, and life along the way. And I get to see it all happening! Now I want to share it with you.

Some say I am the wise old heron. If I am, I think sharing is a wise thing to do. So come into the Perry's backyard with me and see what you can learn too.

Oh, by the way, the Perry family thinks of me as their pet. You can read *The Most Unusual Pet Ever: Henry Our Great Blue Heron and His Adventures* to find out all about that.

I See You

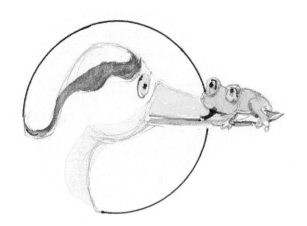

The love that we have for other critters, and the love they have for us, is carried inside our hearts. That love is always with us. When critters do not understand this truth, it leaves them acting and feeling, well . . . let's just say, not quite like themselves.

Mornings are always busy for the frog family that lives in the pond in the Perry's garden. Frog Mom is getting ready to catch breakfast and feed her eight babies. As usual, her littlest, Frog Baby, clings tightly to her leg. With her other frog babies hopping in different directions, she

has to be patient and in charge. Frog Mom is a pro.

"Gather around little ones. Pay attention and watch me catch your breakfast. My mom taught me, and now it's time for you to learn. Soon you will be catching your own breakfast, lunch, and dinner," Frog Mom says as she looks toward the pond. "We have many choices today: flies, insects, and little fish. But catching them takes patience and skill. Now I need all of you to go across the pond, wait quietly, and watch closely. You too, my littlest Frog Baby. I cannot catch anything with you in tow."

"But I want to stay with you!" Frog Baby pleads, hanging on tighter. "I want YOU to watch me! Don't you love me?"

"Of course I do. I love you even when you are across the pond and I cannot touch you," Frog Mom explains gently. "Now please go join your brothers and sisters while I catch breakfast."

"Fine!" Frog Baby sniffles and releases his grip on Frog Mom's leg. He sulks across the pond to a spot all by himself.

"I don't know where he gets the idea that I don't love him unless my eyes are always on him. I love all my little ones, but I only have two eyes and eight babies," Frog Mom says under her breath, taking her position behind a small rock. Soon she hears a fly approaching.

14

Frog Mom whips her tongue out to catch the fly. Suddenly she sees a turtle, hungrily licking his lips, moving toward Frog Baby. Frog Mom quickly abandons the fly, crosses the pond in one giant leap, and lands right in front of the startled turtle. He scurries away as fast as a turtle can go.

"You saved me! You do love me! I thought you were too busy to think about me," Frog Baby yells in delight.

"That's what I've been trying to get you to understand," says Frog Mom. "I love you wherever I am and no matter what I'm doing, always and forever."

"I love you too," Frog Baby says with a *ribbit* and a big smile. He happily joins his sisters and brothers to watch and learn how to catch a meal.

Frog Baby realized that day that constant attention does not equal love. The love his mother has for him is carried in his heart every minute of the day. Her love will always be with him.

It Is What It Is

Who knew that a simple sign saying "Keep Out" could get a lizard so upset? Things do not always go the way we want them to. But critters can choose to be happy anyway.

"Come on family!" shouts Papa Lizard joyfully. "It's a beautiful morning in the Perry's garden. The sun is bright, the sky is blue, the air is warm, and all the flowers are in bloom. Let's get to the pond."

The lizard family begins walking to their favorite spot across the garden.

"I can't wait to lie down on the warm rocks all day," Mother Lizard says dreamily.

"I want to drink from the splashing waterfall and catch bugs," adds Papa Lizard.

"I'm going to swim all day long!" Little Middle Lizard exclaims.

"Let's play Marco Polo," Brother and Sister Lizard chime in together.

Finally the lizard family arrives at the pond.

"Here we are," says Papa Lizard. "What's this? A sign. It says KEEP OUT."

"What?" cries Little Middle Lizard. "This is horrible. What are we going to do all day? Why would they close the pond? No!" he screams.

"There are plenty of other places to play and things to do," says Papa Lizard. "Look, your brother has already found a suitable rock to practice his pushups, and your sister is happily rolling in that mud puddle."

"How can they just go on having fun? It's not fair," fumes Little Middle Lizard. "My whole day is ruined."

Papa Lizard simply shakes his head and begins hunting for bugs.

Little Middle Lizard is intent on staying mad. He sulks under the "Keep Out" sign.

More than an hour passes when Little Middle Lizard is startled by a sound from across the garden. Raven, one of the resident chickens, is stirring up the dirt.

"What are you doing?" Little Middle Lizard yells across the garden. "Why are you flapping your wings like that?"

"I'm about to begin a race!" Raven yells back.

"A race? With whom? I don't see any other critters."

"With myself!" declares Raven.

Raven takes off running full speed around the outer edge of the garden. Her wings, legs, and feathers are flying.

"You're too funny!" Little Middle Lizard says, laughing uncontrollably.

In his amusement watching Raven race toward the finish, Little Middle Lizard forgot all about the "Keep Out" sign.

"Thank you, Raven!" he calls out.

"Glad to help. I was tired of watching you pout," says Raven, out of breath. "I know the pond is your favorite place, but we can't change that it's closed."

"You're right. It is what it is. I won't let it ruin my day," replies Little Middle Lizard as he joins Raven for the next race.

Little Middle Lizard thankfully realized that some things just are what they are, and life is what you make of it. He could not open up the pond, but he could change his attitude and still enjoy the beautiful day.

More, More, More!

Even critters need to be reminded that there is enough of everything for all of us. Sometimes the more we go after, the less we end up with.

It's spring! The flowers and trees are blooming. The sun is shining, and the pond's waterfall is overflowing. There is plenty of bird seed in the feeders and lots of slimy worms too. It's a fun time of year in the Perry's garden. The birds have so much to share as they catch up from being gone all winter.

"Look at my cute Little Robin. She is so excited," Mother Robin says proudly. "It's her first time seeing so many yummy worms."

"I can't believe it! Look at all the worms!" Little Robin exclaims, gobbling as fast as she can. "But I

better catch worms first and eat later. If I eat them as I go, I won't get as many," she figures, and begins moving faster and faster.

"What are you doing?" asks Mother Robin.

"I'm trying to gather as many worms as I can for myself," Little Robin pants. "I'm piling them up here, away from the others. They are for me to have later."

"I see," says Mother Robin, as she watches her cute little one become a little too excited.

"My pile is **NOT** getting bigger! No matter how many worms I add, they keep crawling away!" Little Robin cries out angrily. "Move!" she shouts, pushing one of her sisters out of the way to snatch the worm dangling from another bird's mouth.

"More, more, more!" Little Robin chants loudly.

"Hey Little Robin, there is plenty for all of us," the other birds chirp.

Little Robin ignores them and continues, frantically gathering worms.

Mother Robin has seen enough. She pulls Little Robin aside. "We have this wonderful garden with plenty of worms for everyone. But your greedy behavior shows no respect for the others, and no appreciation for the garden!" scolds Mother Robin. "If you could be glad for your sisters and the others when they caught a worm, you would be enjoying yourself now instead of feeling so frantic."

Little Robin bows her head. "I'm sorry, Mother. There are so many worms. I thought I needed to have them all. Is that what greed is?"

"Yes," Mother Robin replies.

Little Robin carries the few worms left in her pile over to her sisters for them to enjoy.

"I feel better now," she sighs.

When we put our effort and energy into greedy behavior, the situation never goes well. It is always better to be happy for other critters in their good fortune and share ours with them.

Even a Turkey Can Get Up a Tree

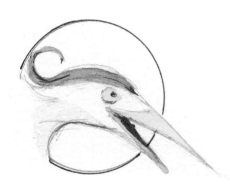

We can be our own worst enemy if we're telling ourselves negative things. We are not able to soar when our heads are filled with doubt.

You can hear them before you see them . . . *gobble, gobble, gobble.* It's the turkeys! They're always a delight. Many of us critters have been curious for a while about Young Male Turkey's behavior. Whenever the flock roams the neighborhood, he's always up in front running ahead of all the other turkeys and flapping his wings madly.

"Come on! Come on!" shouts Young Male Turkey to the flock following slowly behind.

"You go ahead and run. Flap those wings as hard as you like," the eldest turkey replies. "Why are you in such a hurry anyway?"

"I'm not in a hurry. I'm getting my legs and wings ready. I want to practice every chance I get," Young Male Turkey says proudly.

"What are you practicing for?"

"I want to fly up into the trees one day! I can picture it. What a great view I'll have," he explains excitedly.

"Turkeys can't fly! Every turkey knows this. You should stop dreaming," says the eldest turkey sternly, shaking his head.

"That's what the whole flock keeps telling me," Young Male Turkey says softly. "It doesn't matter. I should still try," he tells himself. He continues practicing anyway.

"Come on legs, run! Come on wings, flap! Why does this happen every time I tell the flock that I want to fly?" Young Male Turkey ponders.

He hangs his head low. "Maybe I shouldn't think about flying into the trees. Maybe my legs and wings won't ever get me up there," he gobbles sadly. "Turkeys can't fly. Turkeys can't fly," he repeats to himself, over and over.

The afternoon passes. As the turkeys stroll down the middle of the road, they are startled by a loud, fast car heading in their direction.

"Car coming! Get out of the way!" screams the flock, gobbling frantically.

There is no time to think! The turkeys scatter everywhere fast.

After the car streaks by and it is safe, the flock regroups on the side of the road.

"Why do cars have to go so fast? At my age it's getting harder to move so quickly," the eldest turkey grumbles, out of breath. "Hey, where is Young Male Turkey? He was up in front before the car nearly ran us over."

"I'm up here!" shouts Young Male Turkey from the top of a nearby tree. "I knew I could do it! I knew it!" he says, bursting with joy.

All the turkeys begin to run through the neighborhood, gobbling in excitement, happy that Young Male Turkey reached his dream.

Because Young Male Turkey had to react quickly, he had no time to think. When the negative thoughts filling his head suddenly disappeared, he was finally able to get out of his own way and fly. You see, even a turkey can make it up a tree if he stops telling himself that he can't.

Give a Hug, Get a Hug

It makes no difference whether you have feathers or fur. Every critter wants to be loved and understood. On this day Mr. Duck and Baby Squirrel, a very unlikely pair, learn how alike they really are and that a simple hug can be magical.

"What's Baby Squirrel doing next to my pond, pouting behind that bush?" Mr. Duck wonders. Baby Squirrel is usually jumping from tree to tree, laughing and chasing his brother, their furry tails flapping wildly.

Curious, Mr. Duck waddles over to ask Baby Squirrel.

"Okay, spill it," quacks Mr. Duck. "This isn't like you. Why aren't you running around making a bunch of noise? Where is your brother?"

"He's gone," Baby Squirrel sniffles.

"Gone? Gone where?" asks Mr. Duck.

"My brother moved to a neighborhood down the road. He has a family now. It's not too far away. He says he'll visit, but I miss him. I'm afraid he'll forget about me," Baby Squirrel explains sadly.

A surprising feeling wells up inside Mr. Duck.

"Oh," says Mr. Duck softly, waddling closer toward Baby Squirrel. "The same thing happened to me when I was your age. My older brother moved to a different pond at the park when he got a family of his own. I missed my brother very much at first. I was also afraid that he would forget about me."

"Really?" asks Baby Squirrel. He wipes his tears and stands a little straighter.

"Yes, but I've seen you and your brother together. He will miss you too. He will visit and be very happy to see you. You and your brother will still have as much fun as always, just like me and my brother did," says Mr. Duck.

"You think so?"

"Don't worry, it's going to be okay. I promise."

"Thank you, Mr. Duck. I never knew you were so kind," says Baby Squirrel.

"Any time," replies Mr. Duck as he stretches out his wing and wraps it around Baby Squirrel.

"A hug," Baby Squirrel sighs and nestles his head inside Mr. Duck's wing. "This is nice. I feel better."

"I do too," says Mr. Duck happily.

Mr. Duck and Baby Squirrel felt the magic of a simple hug. That is, when you give a hug, you also get one back. A light touch, a kind word, a simple smile . . . these are the things that truly

matter. One critter might have feathers and the other fur, but both want to be loved and comforted.

Bratty Blue Jays?

There are many different critters that hang out in the Perry's garden, and they all have their own behaviors. Sometimes critters can act so differently that it's tempting to judge them quickly based on a single behavior. But it's always better to be patient and get to know someone.

On this foggy fall morning, lots of different birds are sharing the Perry's garden: sparrows, finches, robins, doves, quails, chickens, and blue jays.

The finches gather at the bird feeder. "Good morning sparrows," the finches chirp cheerfully. "Did you have a good night?"

"No. The strong wind was blowing through our nests all night long. And it was cold."

"Oh, you sparrows always have something to complain about," the finches joke. "But we know that's just your way."

Meanwhile, the quail family begins hopping over the fence one by one, making their way to the bird feeder. And the dove family swoops down from the roof to join them.

"Good morning quails and doves," chirp the sparrows and finches. "Do you want your breakfast on the ground today, or do you want a turn at the feeder?"

"Very funny. You know we like to eat our seed on the ground. Will you please push some out of the feeder for us?"

"Here it comes!"

Then the robins arrive in the garden and wait patiently for their turn at the feeder.

"Go ahead, robins, your turn," chirp the sparrows and finches as they fly off the feeder.

One of the robins looks at the quails eating on the ground below. "I know you quails can fly, but I see you fast-walking everywhere. Why?"

34

asks the robin, teasing.

"Because we like to!" The quails respond.

"I know, I know," says the robin with a smile.

"The blue jays will be showing up soon," warns one of the chickens from under the feeder. "Better eat up! The blue jays don't know how to wait their turn."

"I think you mean the bratty blue jays," says another chicken. "They can clear the garden out with one loud *squawk!* None of us sounds like they do. I don't like it."

All the birds in the garden nod in agreement.

"Here they come! Get off the feeder now!" the chickens cluck loudly.

Two squawking blue jays swoop into the garden and land on the empty feeder.

"I don't know why all the birds leave when we arrive," says one of the blue jays.

"Well, at least we don't have to wait in line!" says the other blue jay, turning his head to laugh. "Hey, do you see the red-tailed hawk perched high in that tree?"

"I do now. He's looking for his breakfast, and I don't think he wants

bird seed," replies the blue jay. "Oh no! He's got his sights on the little birds in the garden!"

As both blue jays realize what is about to happen, they loudly begin alerting the other birds. "*Squawk! Squawk! Squawk! Hide!*"

The birds scatter throughout the garden to hide until the danger passes.

Every bird was safe, thanks to the blue jays and their loud squawking.

"I guess we should have gotten to know these blue jays better," says one of the chickens. "Actually, they're pretty cool. They saved us."

All the birds in the garden nod in agreement.

The birds learned that the blue jays' loud squawking actually protects them. They learned that it isn't good to make judgments based on one behavior. When we make quick judgments, we miss out on the good stuff that every critter has to offer.

Wings That Won't Fly

Some critters have four legs. Others have two. Some critters can see in the dark. Others can smell a critter coming miles away. All critters have their own special talents and traits. Being different is a good thing.

All three of the resident chickens are hungry. They are eager to get from their coop into the garden to see what has been left for their breakfast.

"Are you ready? Are you ready?" clucks Raven as she prepares herself. "The coop gate will be opened soon. I'm going to be the first to get to the garden today!"

"Yes, Raven. We're ready," clucks Braveheart, the youngest of the three chickens, rolling her eyes.

"Mother, are you ready? I can hear footsteps!"

"Raven, would you stop asking?" clucks Mother, the eldest chicken. "We go through this every morning. Every morning we race. And every morning you win. We know your wings are the strongest. Stop pestering us! Here comes Mr. Perry."

Mr. Perry opens the coop, and the three chickens run out.

Raven gets to the garden first. "I win!" she declares. "Oh look, we have watermelon for breakfast! My favorite."

"Yes, you win again," clucks Mother and Braveheart. They arrive behind Raven and begin enjoying the delicious watermelon.

It's early but already the garden is full with birds looking for their breakfast.

"Hello chickens," the red robins chirp.

"Hello little birds," the chickens cluck.

"Last night was so windy!" complains one of the red robins. "We had to change resting places four times before we found a warm spot."

"I didn't feel the wind," says Raven.

"You're lucky because you have fluffy wings. Of course you didn't feel it," says one of the robins.

After a few minutes, the red robins gather to leave. "It's time for us to go and see what the other bird feeders in the neighborhood have today. No one brings us watermelon. See you again tomorrow," the red robins chirp, and fly out of the garden together.

"Bye," says Raven. "I wish I could go along," she thinks to herself, watching them all leave.

Then the doves arrive and land next to the chickens.

"Good morning," they coo.

"Good morning," reply the chickens, who are now scratching in the dirt looking for bugs and worms to eat.

"Did you hear that owl last night?" the doves ask.

"No. It's hard to hear inside the chicken coop," Raven says.

"Lucky for you! We were so afraid that the owl would eat us for dinner."

The doves spend a short time eating and then prepare to leave.

"We hate to eat and run, but it's time for us to go," says one of the doves.

"Where are you going?" Raven asks anxiously.

"We are looking for a safer nesting spot, away from the owl. We do not have a coop."

"Okay, good-bye then," Raven says sadly. She watches the doves fly out of the garden together.

"Not fair!" Raven clucks loudly. "Why can't I come and go like the other birds can? It's my wings. They aren't the flying kind. I want to be like the flying birds. I want to be free!"

Raven spreads one of her wings and looks at it with displeasure.

"Think about what you're saying," Mother clucks at Raven. "If you were a wild bird and could fly out of here, you would have to find a spot to sleep every night with danger lurking all around. There wouldn't be a coop to run to. Wild flying birds don't have

coops. And would you want to hunt for your own food each day, never knowing what you might find or not find? That would mean no more watermelon."

"I didn't think about all that," Raven says. "I'm not that kind of bird. I don't think I could survive."

"That's right Raven. And it's those wings you're frowning at that keep you so warm at night. Your strong wings are what wins you the race every morning," Mother says in a gentle tone.

"Thank you for the reminder, Mother," Raven clucks. She stands up tall and kisses each of her wings.

Then Raven takes off running, flapping her wings wildly as she attempts to squawk *cock-a-doodle-do.*

"That's our Raven!" Mother and Braveheart cluck together. "She's not a rooster, but when she acts like one, we know she's happy."

Raven embraced herself for who she is. She accepted her wings and realized the safety and goodness they provide. Critters should not compare themselves to other critters. We all have different talents and traits. Thank goodness that we do!

Me Too!

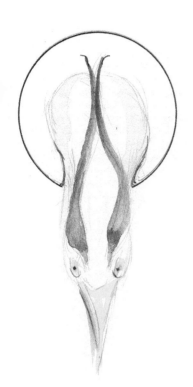

No matter if they are a lizard, a bird, or a squirrel, all little ones experience times of awkwardness. They think they are the only ones to feel that way and that no one else could possibly understand.

I have been visiting the Perry's garden for over ten years now. I have seen lots of babies born, and have had the pleasure of watching them grow up and go on to make families and lives of their own. Every year I invite all the little ones to the garden so I can share my own story about the time when I was a little one and felt awkward and alone.

This year I invited Baby Squirrel, Little Frog, the lizard kids, some baby chicks, and a few new songbirds. I cleared an area in the middle of the garden and asked the critters to sit in a circle facing outward, so they could feel more at ease raising their hands and answering questions. Their parents would be coming back in one hour to get them.

Standing in the middle of the circle, I begin to tell my story.

"When I was a young great blue heron I felt that everyone looked at me a little funny. I was very tall at an early age. I didn't feel as smart as the other herons, and I wasn't sure how to make friends. I felt that no one really liked me."

After a while, I ask everyone in the circle to close their eyes. "Raise your hand if you ever feel the same way I did. Now keep your hand up, open your eyes, and look around."

As the little ones look around the circle, their eyes and mouths open wide. Every critter's hand is raised! With amazement, the little ones realize that they are not alone with their feelings.

This is my favorite part, watching and listening as the little ones eagerly open up and share.

"We feel awkward because our feathers haven't all grown in yet, and our necks are too tall for our bodies!" the baby chicks squeal.

"I feel timid around other squirrels because I'm still nervous about climbing so far up the tree to my house," Baby Squirrel says.

"We have feelings too!" shout the lizard kids, jumping up and down. "Our skin sheds, and sometimes others look at us funny."

"Everyone is bigger than us!" cry Little Frog and the songbirds.

All the little ones are talking at the same time. It's a wonderful sound.

When the talking calms down, I continued. "As I grew up, little by little, the awkwardness began to melt away, and my feelings started to change. When you're young, every moment is an opportunity for growing, learning, understanding, and experiencing new things. We all eventually grow into our bodies and make friends. It just takes time. And remember, everyone goes through it!"

All the little ones are relieved, as if they had been told a special secret.

Sharing our feelings can be nothing short of a miracle. Connecting with others helps us understand ourselves. When we keep our thoughts and feelings to ourselves, we feel lonely. When we share, we learn how alike we all are. Every feeling, good or bad, has been felt by many other critters before us. So don't be too hard on yourself.

Painting a Picture with Choices

*Sometimes the best way to learn how to behave is to observe how **NOT** to behave. Recently some of my dearest critter friends and I got a firsthand look at children acting poorly. If they could have seen themselves as we did, surely they would have chosen to behave much better.*

It was late in the afternoon. I had been taking a nap next to the pond. My dear friends, after a full day of play, were resting with me: the dove girls, Elise, Daphne, and Emma; the red robin boys, Bryce and Ryan; the squirrel sisters, Anna, Paula, and Julia; and Dylan the red cardinal.

"What a fun day. Thanks for inviting us over, Henry," Elise, Daphne, and Emma, the doves, cooed softly, waking up from their nap.

"What a great picnic we had," Anna, Paula, and Julia, the squirrel sisters, added as they got up and stretched.

"We should do this again soon. We can play so many more games when we're all together," cheered Bryce and Ryan, the red robins, and Dylan, the red cardinal.

Suddenly we were startled by horrible sounds of fussing and ranting. We scurried to the fence where the noise was coming from, and wrangled for a good spot to peek at what was causing all the commotion. It was a human family with two children, a young boy and girl. The parents were trying to get them in the car, but the children resisted.

"Why do we have to go with you? We don't want to!" they screamed. Their faces turned mean as they twisted their bodies to prevent their parents from putting them in the car. "Let us stay here! We are old enough to stay home!" they begged and pleaded loudly. "You're the meanest parents ever!"

My critter friends and I were astonished by the dreadful behavior.

"Just by the way those kids are acting you can see they are not mature enough to be left alone," whispered the doves, Elise, Daphne, and Emma.

"No kidding. I would never act that way to my parents, or to anyone," Dylan, the red cardinal, added.

"Do those kids think they are going to get their way with that kind of behavior?" Anna, Paula, and Julia, the squirrel sisters, wondered out loud.

"Screaming and saying mean words won't get your parents to listen to you," Bryce, one of the red robins, declared.

"Neither will kicking and hitting," added Ryan, the other red robin.

"Even though the kids are young, they are still old enough to make choices about how to behave," the first dove, Elise, proclaimed.

"They could talk nicely to their parents and explain what they want in a calm voice," said Daphne, the second dove. "Then their parents might listen."

"And those faces! It's hard to show your maturity when your face is red and tight with anger," Emma, the third dove, added without taking her eyes off the commotion.

The critters all looked at each other and shook their heads.

Then the squirrel sisters, Anna, Paula, and Julia said aloud what we were all thinking. "We never want to be seen acting like that."

We slowly walked back to the pond as the car drove away with the children still screaming in the back seat.

Actions really do speak louder than words. Every day we can choose how to behave. What is the look on your face? Where are your hands? What is the tone of your voice? How are you standing? These choices of behavior paint a picture of ourselves for others to see.

Twilight Song of Thanks and Gratitude

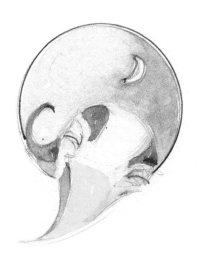

My favorite part of the day is just after the sun goes down. At first it's quiet as all the critters settle in for the night. Then the gentle humming begins. So many little thoughts of thanks and gratitude are felt and sung, making the prettiest of sounds.

The critters are thanking the sun and the stars and the moon, grateful for the comfortable nest, hole, or bush they call home. Thankful for the food they had today, and for the water that washes them and quenches their thirst. For the wind and the rain, the grass and the trees, and all the beautiful flowers in the Perry's garden.

We are grateful for each other and for all the bugs and butterflies too. Thank you! Thank you! Thank you!

With an attitude of gratitude I smile hearing the chickens coo, the frogs ribbit, the owls hoot, and the crickets chirp. And all is well. Tomorrow is another day to enjoy the gift of nature's beauty and bounty.

The critters know that we are presented with amazing wonders every day. Celebrate, with a thankful spirit, all these wonders, including the sun, the stars, the moon, and YOU!

About the Author

Sondra Perry lives in San Ramon, California, with her husband Lance. Her first book, "The Most Unusual Pet Ever: Henry Our Great Blue Heron and His Adventures," is the true story of meeting "Henry the Heron" and their continued friendship. This is the first book in the "Kids Carrots Book Series." Look for the second book in the series, *Crunchy Carrots*, coming out in 2014. Sondra is available for readings and gives fun and educational presentations to groups of all ages. You can reach her at sondra.perry4@gmail.com.

About the Illustrator

Award-winning artist Janice Byer has a Bachelor of Fine Arts degree from the California College of Arts and Crafts. She is a successful watercolor, pastel, and oil painter. Visit her online at www.artistjanicebyer.com.

Please visit

www.KidsCarrotsBookSeries.com

or

www.HenryTheGreatBlueHeron.com

for more information and to see pictures of

Henry and some of the other critters from the stories.

Henry the Great Blue Heron